Here Come the Holidays!

Stories and Poems

illustrated by David Wenzel

SCHOLASTIC INC.

New York   Toronto   London   Auckland   Sydney
Mexico City   New Delhi   Hong Kong   Buenos Aires

ISBN 0-439-80005-6

Designed by Jennifer Rinaldi Windau

12 11 10 9 8 7 6 5 4   5 6 7 8 9 10/0
Printed in the U.S.A.   40

First Scholastic printing, November 2005

CONTENTS

TWO POEMS

by Jack Prelutsky

IT'S CHRISTMAS

It's Christmas! Merry Christmas!
Yes, it's merry, merry Christmas,
it's time for hanging stockings,
it's time for riding sleighs,
it's time for jolly greeting,
snow and holly, overeating,
oh, I love you Merry Christmas
you're the best of holidays.

OUR CHRISTMAS PLAY

We were nervous and excited
in assembly today,
for our parents came to visit us,
and watch our Christmas play.

Our teachers helped a little,
but we did the most ourselves,
the fattest kid played Santa
and the smallest kids were elves.

A few were Santa's reindeer
so they got to run and leap,
some of us were shepherds,
and a bunch were woolly sheep,
there was Jesus in the manger,
there were angels wearing wings,
there was Joseph, there was Mary,
And the three wise Eastern kings.

We wore makeup, we wore costumes,
it was really lots of fun,
and our parents all applauded
when our Christmas play was done,
then we took our bows together,
everyone that is, but me —

I just stood there, green and fragrant,
for I played the Christmas tree.

ZOMBIES DON'T MAKE CHRISTMAS CANDY

by Debbie Dadey and Marcia Thornton Jones

"What is that smell?" Eddie asked. He held his stomach and drew in a breath as big as the North Pole. "I'm so hungry I could eat a reindeer!"

Eddie and his three friends Howie, Liza, and Melody were walking home from Bailey Elementary School. Snow danced through the air and stuck to their eyelashes.

Melody laughed and tossed the snow from her black braids. "Santa would not like it if you slurped down Rudolph."

Liza pointed to a small building between the Five and Dime and the Burger Doodle restaurant. "I've never noticed that place before."

"Me, neither," Howie said, looking at the short green building with a bright red and green awning. A sign in the window said CHRISTMAS CANDY SHOPPE.

"It must be new," Eddie said. "There's no way I would miss a candy store."

Melody knew that Eddie loved candy more than Santa loved the North Pole. "That delicious smell is coming from there," she said.

"Let's check it out," Eddie said, reaching for the silver door handle.

"Wait," Liza warned her friends. "Something is not right."

Eddie did not like to wait. Especially when candy was involved. He jerked open the door and got the surprise of his life.

"Yikes!" Eddie screamed.

Standing in front of the four kids was a most unusual person. He wore tight black, shiny pants and a hooded black sweatshirt. His face was pale white, but his fingernails were painted blacker than night.

"Welcome to my candy store," the stranger said. "I am Lester Graves."

Liza gasped. There was something about that name that made her shiver as if someone had slipped a snowball down her neck.

Eddie didn't notice. "Your candy smells great," he said. He licked his lips and looked at the mounds of homemade candy in the display cases. "Do you give free samples?"

Mr. Graves grinned at Eddie. "Why, of

course." As soon as Lester pulled out a tray, Eddie grabbed a handful of candy.

Liza put her hand out to stop Eddie. "No, it's bad for your teeth," she warned. Eddie didn't care about his teeth. He just wanted some of that delicious-smelling candy. He popped it into his mouth and closed his eyes.

"Eddie," Melody warned, "that's not polite."

"Who cares about polite?" Eddie asked around a mouthful of chocolate.

"You should," Howie whispered. "Especially since it's so close to Christmas. If you're not good, you won't get the things on your list."

"My list!" Eddie blurted. Then he bent over and dug deep into his book bag. He pulled out a notebook and turned to the last page.

Melody looked over his shoulder. "What are you doing?" she asked.

"I'm adding chocolate to my Christmas list,"

Eddie told her. "Lots and lots of chocolate. I have to write down everything." Eddie scribbled the word *chocolate* on his list and then stuffed his mouth with more free samples. He closed his eyes, and his face got very pale.

"Eddie," Liza shrieked. "Are you all right?"

Liza was very quiet after the kids left the candy store. Eddie didn't notice. He was too busy chewing caramel covered with gooey chocolate. His face was losing all its color, but that didn't stop Eddie from chomping away on the free candy.

Howie and Melody had been friends with Liza for a long, long time. They knew something was bothering her. Something big. "What's wrong?" asked Melody.

Liza stopped at the corner. She waited so

long that a fine dusting of snow collected on her stocking cap. "We have a problem," she said. "A zombie problem."

"What?" Eddie blurted, except his mouth was still full of candy, so it sounded more like "blup?"

"Didn't you recognize Lester's name?" she asked. "It's Graves. As in Coach Graves."

At the sound of their former soccer coach's name, Howie's face turned as gray as the slushy snow on the sidewalk. Melody gasped.

"So the new guy in town is related to our old soccer coach," Eddie said. "Big deal."

"It is a big deal," Liza said, "if it's a family of zombies."

"We never proved Coach Graves was a zombie," Howie said softly.

"And we never proved she wasn't," Melody

added, remembering that their coach had left town after they had given her salty potato chips. Salt was supposed to get rid of zombies.

"Who cares about zombies?" Eddie asked. "This new guy makes great candy."

Liza poked Eddie. "You should care," she said, digging her finger into his chest with each word. "Your face is so pale, maybe you're turning into a zombie. Besides, a zombie has to have a reason for being here, and I think I know what it is."

"You can't be serious," Eddie said.

But Liza was serious. Deadly serious.

For the rest of the week, Liza made her friends spy on Lester's Christmas Candy Shoppe. Day in and day out, shoppers entered the store. And day in and day out, they left the store loaded with packages. But Liza wouldn't let Eddie eat another bite of Lester Graves' chocolate.

"Don't you see what Lester's doing?" Liza asked.

"Yeah," Eddie said. "He's making a ton of money by making the best chocolate in the world. What's worse is that we could be eating it if it weren't for you!"

"If it weren't for me, you would be a zombie before Christmas," Liza said. "I think Lester is using the candy to turn people into zombies. The more you eat, the more you want. Pretty soon, Lester has complete control over you."

Howie tugged on Eddie's coat sleeve. "Isn't that your grandmother coming down the sidewalk?" he asked.

Eddie's grandmother was so bundled up in her coat and scarf that it was hard to recognize her. But when she went into Lester's candy store and pulled off her fuzzy cap, the kids knew. "I have to show her what to buy," Eddie said, jerking away from Howie. Eddie looked both ways and then ran across the street.

"No!" Liza screamed, but Eddie's mind was not on zombies. His head was filled with thoughts of chewy candy, crunchy candy, and soft, buttery candy.

"We have to go after him," Liza said.

"You're right," Melody told her.

"You mean you believe Lester is a zombie, too?" Liza asked.

"Of course not," Melody said. "But if we go over there, Eddie's grandmother might buy us an early Christmas treat."

Howie and Melody didn't wait for Liza to argue. They hurried after Eddie. Liza had no choice but to follow.

The inside of the shop was warm compared to the bitter winter wind outside. The store was crowded with shoppers peering into the glass cases full of candy. Their faces were pale.

Lester stood behind the counter. His hood was pulled over his head so it was hard to see his pale face. It made Liza afraid. Very afraid.

"When I found out about this shop, I just had to check it out," Eddie's grandmother explained.

Eddie hadn't even given Lester a second glance. "If you're shopping, then you'll need my list," Eddie told his grandmother. Eddie let his book bag fall to the floor with a thump. He dug deep inside, pulled out his notebook, and handed it to his grandmother.

Eddie's grandmother flipped through the pages. "Which page is your list?" she asked.

Eddie looked confused. "All of them."

"You filled an entire notebook with things you want for Christmas?" Melody asked. Eddie just shrugged his shoulders.

Eddie's grandmother tried to smooth down one of Eddie's red curls. "How about if we just make it a sweet Christmas?" she asked. "I'll buy you a box of this wonderful chocolate!"

"And what else?" Eddie asked.

Eddie's grandmother laughed as she popped a free sample into her mouth. "Nothing else," she said. "The chocolate Mr. Graves makes is all we need for Christmas."

Eddie looked at his grandmother. He looked at the little box of chocolate in her hands. "One stinking box of chocolate?" he blurted. "Is that all? Are you nuts?"

"Nuts?" his grandmother repeated. "Nuts! Chocolate with nuts! That's what we need!"

Before Eddie could argue, his grandmother rushed to a display of chocolate-covered nuts. The rest of the people in the store followed. Eddie looked at his three friends. "This is terrible," he said.

"It's worse than terrible," Liza said. "Look!"

Everyone in the store stared at the candy with the same blank expressions. They were all eating the free samples. The more they chewed, the paler their faces became.

It took every ounce of strength that Liza had, but she pulled her friends out of the store and stood beside the window display. She pointed at the people inside the store. "See? The candy is turning everyone into zombies."

Eddie stopped complaining and spat the candy out of his mouth. The sight of his grandmother staring into space was bad enough, but the thought of getting nothing but candy for

Christmas made him stomp his foot in the snow. Eddie liked candy, but he liked toys just as much. "We have to stop this candy zombie before it's too late," he said.

Howie and Melody nodded their heads. Liza pulled them closer. "This is what we have to do."

As soon as Lester's store opened the next morning, the four kids walked inside the door. Eddie's grandmother and many other customers followed them inside.

"Greetings, young friends," Lester said. "Would you like another free sample?"

Liza shook her head. "No, we brought *you* a free sample. We made candy ourselves last night."

Lester smiled and picked up a piece of the white candy that Liza offered. "Thank you," he said, then popped the soft candy into his mouth.

His eyes got big and then bigger. His hood fell off his head, and he ran from the store.

Eddie's grandmother came up beside him and wagged her finger in his face. "What did you put in that candy?" she asked. "Vinegar?"

Eddie and his three friends shook their heads.

"Poison?" asked Mr. Cooper from the library.

"Of course not," Liza said.

"What was wrong with that candy?" Eddie's grandmother asked.

"Nothing," Liza said with a smile. "Except I may have put in a dash too much salt."

Meadow Mouse and the Christmas-Tree Adventure

by Megan McDonald

Far, far north, in the land beyond trees, lived Meadow Mouse. Down a long tunnel beneath the snow on the meadow, Meadow Mouse made a nest of soft feathers. She spent the winter eating the cotton-grass roots she had stored in nice, neat rows.

One day just before Christmas, Meadow

Mouse felt the ground above her nest shake. It wasn't an earthquake. It was an old woman carrying a lumpy sack. Grandmother was looking for cotton-grass roots. She stepped on the ceiling of Meadow Mouse's nest. The ceiling caved in! When the woman's big furry boot came crashing in, Meadow Mouse raced out through her mouse hole.

She needed a place to hide — quick! Meadow Mouse dashed this way and that, looking for a place that was dark and safe. She ran right into the old woman's sack, which was filled with cotton-grass roots.

Sik-sik-sik. Meadow Mouse nibbled the roots. She liked the new nest! Then . . . *zip!* Quick as a shooting star, Meadow Mouse felt the new nest moving.

Grandmother had picked up her sack and was walking away. She carried the sack over her shoulder. Meadow Mouse peeked out of a tiny hole. The ground rushed past in a blur. Meadow Mouse was flying! She felt dizzy. She didn't like the new nest now!

Meadow Mouse held on tight until the moving stopped. Then *thunk!* The sack landed with a crash on Grandmother's kitchen table.

The old woman got out a big bowl and a mixing spoon. She got a knife and a cutting board. She reached into the bag and took out some roots. (Luckily she did not see Meadow Mouse!)

Wak-wak-wak-wak-wak. Grandmother began chopping the roots. She tossed them into the big bowl, adding three kinds of berries she had been saving in the freezer — cranberries, cloudberries, and crowberries. Next she stirred the roots and berries into some sweet cream and sugar. Christmas would not be Christmas without her special three-berry ice cream. When she was done, Grandmother set the mixture in the freezer and went to warm her feet by the fire.

Meadow Mouse pawed at the sack's small hole, squeezing herself out. Some sugar had spilled on the table. *Mww-mww-mww!* Meadow Mouse licked it up. She licked the ice-cream spoon, too.

Meadow Mouse leaped to the countertop, skidding on the slick surface. A shiny creature glared at her without blinking. Meadow Mouse sniffed at it. Then she climbed up the creature's side. *Aiieee!* This creature had not one mouth, but two! She knew the teeth of a wolverine, but she had never seen the jaws of a toaster. *Eek!* Meadow Mouse raced down the toaster. She slid across the countertop, right into the open silverware drawer.

She ran to the back of the drawer. Then she stopped in her tracks. What was that sound she heard? It was a tiny squeaking sound. House Mouse!

House Mouse peeked out from behind a fork. *Mww-mww-mww!* The two mice squeaked with high-pitched kissing sounds. They sniffed each other and rubbed noses, whiskers twitching.

Just then a giant hand reached into the drawer. House Mouse squeezed out of the drawer through a small hole, Meadow Mouse at his heels. They raced along dusty pipes and wires inside the wall. At last they were safe in House Mouse's home.

Meadow Mouse stared in wonder at the mess of a nest! House Mouse had no soft carpet of grass. He had no walls lined with feathers and no neat rows of cotton-grass roots to feast on. His nest was a terrible tangle of things Meadow Mouse had never seen before. There were bubble-gum wrappers, postage stamps, and half a coffee cup for a bed! Raisins and peanut shells piled topsy-turvy with pop-tops, paper clips, and an old toothbrush. Even a button and three red checkers!

Meadow Mouse could never sleep in such a place. She longed for her peaceful, soft feather bed.

Then House Mouse dragged out a soft, fuzzy slipper from behind the mess. Meadow Mouse and House Mouse curled up in it together, all warm and cozy. It was the perfect bed for a mouse away from home!

Later that night while the old woman dozed in her rocking chair, House Mouse led Meadow Mouse along a secret passageway into the living room. Meadow Mouse saw a tall spruce tree in the room, but it looked different from any tree she had ever seen. It was covered with hundreds of blinking eyes. Had the stars fallen to Earth?

House Mouse raced up the tree. He scampered in and among the stars, filling his cheeks with strands of shiny silver straw. Meadow Mouse jumped onto the tree and found more shiny silver straw, just like House Mouse.

Eeek! Grandmother woke up and chased after the mice. Then a giant broom was sweeping them across the floor, down the hall, and right out the front door into the crisp, cold night!

Meadow Mouse and House Mouse, cheeks bulging, ran until they were far, far away from the big broom and the house.

Soon there was daylight, and Meadow Mouse now led the way. The two friends leaped and chased each other all day, following flocks of snow geese. Then they ran through the night, under the northern lights, heading straight toward the land beyond the trees — back to the meadow.

Weeks later the old woman came back to gather more cotton-grass roots. She pressed her heels lightly into the ground. What was this?

A mouse nest!

Inside she found a wriggling, squirming, squeaking heap of baby mice, all snug in a mouse bed soft and round! But their nest was not made of cotton grass. It was made of bright strands of shiny silver straw — tinsel from her very own Christmas tree!

Grandmother laughed and laughed. Then very gently she covered the nest, good as new, and went on her way.

THE CHRISTMAS CAMEL

by Marisa Montes

More than two thousand years ago, people who lived in the deserts of the Orient and Arabia traveled by foot or on camels. There were two types of camels: In Arabia lived the one-humped camels. In the Orient lived the two-humped camels. Gobi-Kazaam was a two-humped camel.

One day when Gobi was very young, his mother said, "Gobi, our king wants to make friends with King Balthazar of Arabia. He is sending a special gift to King Balthazar — and that gift is you."

Gobi, who loved adventure, began to dance with excitement. Arabia! It must be very far away, for he'd never heard of it. Gobi loved taking long walks. "When shall we go, Mama? How long will it take to get there? Will we ever come back?"

Gobi's mother gazed down at him. Her large, brown eyes filled with tears. "No, Gobi, you will never come back. And you will be going alone, for I cannot go with you."

Gobi stopped dancing and stared at her. "Alone? But — "

"Hush, Gobi, and listen carefully. We do not have much time. You come from a long line of noble camels. Always be proud of who you are. So long as you are good and kind to others, you will be a credit to your family, and I will always be with you."

Young Gobi held up his head and held back his tears. "I will, Mama. I will make you proud."

"I know you will, Gobi, and I know you will be brave. Here are three gifts to help you on your trip."

First Gobi's mother gave him a finely woven blanket of many brilliant colors. "This blanket was worn by your father and his father and his father before him. It will keep you warm on the coldest nights."

Then she gave him a shiny brass locket to clip to one of his furry ears. "This locket contains a salve that will heal any wound. It will keep you well."

Finally she slipped a heavy silver bell from her neck and placed it around her son's neck.

"This bell was my mother's. Its music will bring you comfort and joy."

With that, Gobi's mother led him to the caravan that would take him to Arabia — away from the only home he knew.

The trip to Arabia was long and hard. The hot sun burned, and the strong desert winds blew sand all around. The only things that kept Gobi going were the delicate *tinkle-tinkle-tinkle* of his mother's silver bell and the image of her face shining in his memory.

It took the caravan many weeks to reach the palace of King Balthazar. And when he arrived, Gobi soon found out he was not welcomed.

"A camel with two humps!" The other camels laughed and snickered when Gobi passed by.

Gobi held up his head and said, "I am a noble camel from a noble family." But the others just grunted and spit, as camels will do.

Even the stable hands laughed at Gobi's two humps. King Balthazar, too, was seen shaking his head and grinning. He couldn't believe that the king of the Orient had sent him such an odd gift.

"I promise you, Mama," Gobi whispered to himself, "I will prove myself to all and make you proud."

Gobi began to sneak away from the stables at night before the others could start teasing him. Late one cold night as Gobi wandered alone in the desert, he came upon an old woman. She lay in a heap on the sand, and he wasn't sure whether she was dead or alive.

Gobi poked her gently with his head. The woman rolled over and looked up. "Oh, kind camel, I lost my way, and now I am freezing. Can you carry me home? I am so cold."

Without a second thought, Gobi let his father's blanket slide from his back and placed it over the woman. Then he knelt beside her, and she climbed onto his back. She said that she lived with a tribe of nomads and told Gobi how to get there. He carried the woman to her home. She was still asleep and wrapped in his blanket when her people lifted her from his back. The people thanked Gobi, and he went on his way — without his blanket.

Gobi did not mind. He had long, shaggy hair, and the woman had nothing but bare skin. She needed the blanket more than he did. And he still had the other two gifts to remind him of his mother.

Then one day when Gobi-Kazaam was walking along a road by himself, he found a white dove lying on the ground. Gobi saw that the bird had a broken wing and leg. He bent his head down and told her to take the locket from his ear with her beak. "When you have the locket, open it," Gobi said. "You will find a salve inside. Rub some of it on your wing and leg."

With great effort the dove did as she was told. Soon she was able to stand, but she could not fly. Gobi gave her the locket with the healing salve, and continued on his way. He did not mind. He was strong and healthy, and the dove was not. She needed the locket much more than he did. And Gobi-Kazaam still had his mother's bell to remind him of her.

Many months later Gobi was traveling in a caravan to a far-off city. They came upon a shepherdess and her little son. The boy was crying, his face red and puffy. Try as she might, his mother could not cheer him up. But when Gobi walked by and the *tinkle-tinkle-tinkle* of his silver bell filled the air, the boy stopped crying. He stood still and just stared at the bell around the camel's neck.

Then the little boy smiled and pointed at the bell. Gobi stopped. But when Gobi stopped, the ringing stopped, and the child began to cry again. Gobi shook his head, and the bell tinkled gaily. The boy stopped crying and grinned. His large, sad eyes, still brimming with tears, reminded Gobi of his mother's sad eyes the last time he had seen her. Gobi wanted to stop the child's sadness. So, as much as he loved his mother's bell, he slipped it off his head and into the child's outstretched hand.

The boy shook the bell and laughed. The sound of his laughter mingled with the tinkling of the bell and found a spot in Gobi's heart. The bell was the last of Gobi's mother's gifts — the last thing he had to remind him of her. But the boy needed it more because Gobi had the sound of the bell's tinkling and the child's laughter to hold in his heart.

The other camels said he was foolish to give his silver bell to a strange child. But Gobi paid no attention to them, as he had not paid attention to them before. Someday . . . someday he would have his chance to prove himself.

Years went by. Gobi-Kazaam grew up serving King Balthazar. One day there was exciting news in the palace. The wise King Balthazar had been expecting this news, which had been foretold for centuries. Now the time had come. A King of kings would be born in a distant land. And the greatest of kings would travel to this new King, to pay homage and to bring Him gifts. The kings would follow a star — a brilliant star — that would lead them to the land of Judea. One of the kings would be King Balthazar himself.

This is my chance, thought Gobi. I will carry King Balthazar on the trip to Judea. I will take him there safely to honor the new King. This is my chance to prove myself and to make my mother proud.

When Gobi offered his services to the king, everyone laughed. Even the king looked Gobi up and down, and shook his head in doubt. But Gobi stood proud and tall, and the king was forced to take another look.

"There is something very noble about you, Gobi. You are shorter than my other camels, and you have two humps instead of one. But you are strong, and you have always served me well. I will give you a chance."

And so it was that Gobi-Kazaam became King Balthazar's head camel on the long trek across the desert. The brilliant star shone both day and night, and they followed it to the East.

The trip would take several months over many hundreds of miles. After a few weeks King Balthazar was joined by King Melchior of Ethiopia. Later they met up with King Kasper of the Orient.

At one point in the journey, the kings were warned to turn back. They were about to enter a country that was at war. They would surely be injured or taken captive. But as they talked about what to do, a white dove flew down from the sky and spoke to Gobi-Kazaam: "Fear not, old friend. Go on with your journey, for wherever you go, there shall be peace."

Gobi was overjoyed! This was the dove he had saved so long ago. He trusted her and told the kings to go on. And so they did. And wherever they went, there was peace.

After many weeks the kings began to run low on food. They still had far to go. When they had almost no food left, they came upon another group of travelers — a tribe of nomads. There at the head of the group was an old woman.

The moment the woman saw the camel with two humps, she ran up to him and threw her arms around his neck. "Dear old friend, I remember you! Is there anything I can do for you? Whatever you need is yours."

Gobi knew that she was the woman he had saved that cold night years ago. So he told her what they needed. The nomads filled all the kings' baskets with food — enough to last them until they got to Judea.

Gobi and the three kings continued their trip. The days were so hot that they drank more than usual. Before long they found that there was almost no water in their water jugs. Where would they find water in this hot, lonely desert? Suddenly they heard a tinkling noise — it sounded like water trickling over smooth rocks. Far off they could see a herd of sheep led by a boy carrying a silver bell.

As they approached, the boy turned and stared at the two-humped camel. Could it be? The boy smiled and rang his bell. Yes! The boy was older and taller, but Gobi recognized his mother's silver bell. This was the boy who had been crying with sadness so many years ago!

"Dear camel," said the boy, "is there anything I can do for you?"

Gobi told him the kings needed water. The boy was now a shepherd and knew this part of the desert well. He led them to an oasis that had plenty of water. The kings filled their jugs. Now they had enough water for the rest of the trip to Judea.

For many more days and nights, Gobi and the three kings followed the star. At last it led them to the town of Bethlehem. The star kept moving forward, and finally it stopped above a small stable.

Carrying their gifts of gold and myrrh and frankincense, the kings went into the stable. There they found a man and a woman and a newborn baby, who lay in a manger full of straw. Even though they were in a plain and simple stable, the kings were filled with awe. They fell to their knees and bowed their heads and held out their gifts. For before them in the straw lay the greatest King of all — the King of the Jews — the King of kings.

Gobi-Kazaam's heart burst with joy. He knew that by giving away his mother's gifts, he had helped bring the three kings to honor the new King.

Gobi felt his mother was with him and that she was happy and proud.

AUTHOR'S NOTE

To this day, the visit of the three kings to the baby Jesus is celebrated in Hispanic countries on January 6. It is known as El Día de Reyes, *or "Three Kings Day." Although the celebration of Christmas and the arrival of Santa Claus on December 25 is the big event, the tradition of* Los Reyes Magos *is still important. For example, in Puerto Rico traditional Catholics meet to pray the rosary and to honor the three kings, or Wise Men (saints in the Catholic faith). The children get ready to receive gifts from the three Wise Men by collecting freshly cut grass to put in a shoebox for the Wise Men's camels to eat. Then they place a wish list in the box and slide the box under their beds. In the morning the children wake up early to see what the three kings have brought them.*

MERRY CHRISTMAS! HAPPY HANUKKAH! HARAMBEE!

by Stephanie Calmenson

Holiday lights,
See them shine.
Let's celebrate holidays,
Yours and mine.

It was a snowy Monday in December. The kids in Ms. Meyer's class were making holiday decorations.

"Pass the yellow crayon, please," said Anna.

Anna needed the crayon to color flames on five candles.

"Wait," said Sara. "You don't have enough candles. You need nine."

"No, she doesn't," said Willie. "She needs seven."

"I need five candles," said Anna. "There are five candles in an Advent wreath."

"Candles go in a menorah," said Sara. "And there are nine."

"They go in a kinara," said Willie. "And there are seven."

"You're both wrong," said Anna.

"Are not!" said Sara and Willie.

"Are, too!" said Anna.

"Ms. Meyer! Ms. Meyer!" called the three friends together.

When Ms. Meyer came over, Anna, Sara, and Willie told her their problem.

"I believe you're each right for your own holiday," said Ms. Meyer. "Anna, which holiday do you celebrate?"

"Christmas," said Anna.

"Sara, which is your holiday?" asked Ms. Meyer.

"Hanukkah," said Sara.

"Which.holiday do you celebrate, Willie?" asked Ms. Meyer.

"Kwanzaa," said Willie.

"I am going to give you a homework assignment," said Ms. Meyer.

Sara, Anna, and Willie moaned and groaned. "Ugh!" "No!"

"Don't worry, I'll take away another assignment. I think you'll enjoy this one," said Ms. Meyer.

The kids brightened.

"I'd like each of you to share with the class the story of your holiday. How did it get started? What are some of the traditions? Be sure to tell us about the candles! After your stories have been told, I'll have a surprise for everyone."

Anna, Sara, and Willie definitely liked surprises. And sharing the stories of their holidays really did sound like fun.

They worked on their reports over the next two days. On Wednesday it was Anna's turn to speak to the class.

"My holiday is Christmas," she said. "Christmas is a happy holiday. It's when Christian people celebrate the birth of Jesus Christ. This is how the story goes.

"When Jesus was born in a little town called Bethlehem, an angel appeared before some shepherds announcing his birth. Wise Men called Magi, bearing gifts, followed a bright star to the stable where Jesus lay in a manger.

"Today people celebrate the birth of Jesus in many different ways. Here are some things people do in America:

"Outside churches and homes you might see a crèche. That's one of my favorite things. It's a model of Jesus's cradle surrounded by the people and animals who welcomed Him when He was born.

"Many people hang pretty Christmas wreaths on their doors.

"There are Christmas trees decorated with lights, ornaments, strings of cranberries or popcorn, and tinsel. A star goes on top of the tree to remind us of the star that led the three Wise Men to Jesus.

"Christmas is a time of giving. We give to

people who are less fortunate. We put gifts for family and friends under the Christmas tree. And you know about Santa Claus. Santa Claus used to be called St. Nicholas and is the biggest gift-giver of all!

"We go to church, sing Christmas carols, and send Christmas cards. We have big holiday dinners. If we're lucky we get to have stuffed turkey or ham or goose, mashed potatoes, cranberry sauce, pumpkin pie, plum pudding, fruitcake, and eggnog. Am I making you hungry?

"Now I'll tell you why I had to do this special homework. It started with candles.

"Four weeks before Christmas Day is a time called Advent. Advent means 'the coming of,' as in the coming of Jesus. It begins on a Sunday and ends on Christmas Eve.

"Some families have a beautiful Advent calendar to mark the passing of the days. There is a flap for each day leading to Christmas, and when it's lifted, there is a Christmas picture or verse from the Bible.

"Some families light one Advent candle. It's a candle that has every date of the four weeks written down the side of it. Each night the candle is melted down only as far as the next date.

"My family makes an Advent wreath. It's made of evergreen branches and smells so good. Four candles are set in the branches, one for each Sunday of Advent. On each of the Sundays, we light a candle and say prayers together. The first two candles are purple. The third and fourth candles are pink. On Christmas Day we put one white candle at the center. That candle stands for Jesus. Here is a picture of my family's Advent wreath last year. Isn't it pretty?

"Those are just some of the customs in America. People here and around the world celebrate different ways. But the one thing that stays the same is that Christmas is a happy holiday!"

Anna took a bow just for fun, and everyone clapped.

"That was terrific," said Ms. Meyer. "Thank you."

On Thursday it was Sara's turn to tell her story. She came to school dressed in her best holiday clothes.

"I'm here to tell you about the holiday of Hanukkah," she said. "Hanukkah, the Hebrew word for *dedication*, is the Jewish people's Festival of Lights. The story of the holiday starts a long time ago. It has a sad beginning and a happy ending.

"In the beginning the Jewish people lived

under a wicked ruler, Antiochus, who did not allow Jewish people to follow their traditions. He took over their temple. He even had Jewish people killed. A man named Judas Maccabees helped lead the fight for freedom, and won. When the struggle was over, they decided to rededicate their temple. Inside was a menorah. A menorah is a special candleholder with places for eight candles, plus one more candle, called the *shamash*, that is set apart to light the others. The menorah in the temple had only enough oil to burn for one day, but somehow it lasted for eight days. The holiday of Hanukkah lasts eight days to celebrate this miracle of lights.

"Here are some of the things we do:

"We light our own menorahs. On the first night of Hanukkah, the shamash is lit and used to light one candle. On the second night a new shamash is lit and used to light two candles. The candles are put in right to left and are lit left to right. On the eighth night there are nine lit candles, including the shamash, on the menorah. Here is a collage I made to show you all the candles lit on the eighth night.

"We give gifts to family and friends, and make donations to those who are not as fortunate.

"We eat latkes, which are potato pancakes cooked in oil.

"We play games with a dreidel, which is a spinning top that has a Hebrew letter on each side. The letters put together mean, 'A great miracle happened there.'

"Like Christmas, Hanukkah is a happy holiday."

Ms. Meyer thanked Sara, and everyone clapped for her excellent presentation.

On Friday Willie came to school wearing his holiday colors of red, black, and green. He stood proudly in front of the class and told his story.

"Kwanzaa is an African-American holiday created in 1966 by Dr. Maulana Karenga, a black studies professor living in California. It is a celebration of the history, culture and values of African-Americans.

"Kwanzaa is celebrated in December as a reminder of ancient African harvest and "first fruit" ceremonies. The earth is harvested through teamwork, and the spirit of teamwork is part of the seven principles of Kwanzaa.

"The holiday begins on December 26 and lasts seven days. People who celebrate begin each day with the question, *'Habari Gani?'* which in Swahili means, 'What's the news?'

"Each day the answer to the question is one

of the Seven Principles. *Nguzo Saba* is Swahili for the Seven Principles. The principles are about working together to help ourselves and one another. I know the Swahili words for them, but will just say them in English: unity, self-determination, collective work and responsibility, cooperative economics, purpose, creativity, faith.

"During the holiday, we cover a table with African cloth and put a straw mat called a *mkeka* on it. A special candleholder called a *kinara* goes on this table. The kinara holds seven candles: one black candle, three red, and three green. The black candle, which stands for unity, is at the center of the kinara and is lit the first day. One more candle is lit each day from left to right, starting with the red candles. The candles stand for the Seven Principles. After we light the candles, we talk about the principle of the day. Then we all call out, *'Harambee!'* which means, 'Let's pull together!' We call out once on the first day, twice on the second, all the way to seven times in a row on the seventh day. 'Harambee! Harambee!'

"There is a lot more to tell you about our holiday. For example we eat delicious food and give special presents. But I mostly wanted to tell you what the holiday's about and introduce the kinara, with its seven candles, because that's how this whole report got started!"

"Excellent job, Willie!" said Ms. Meyer as his classmates clapped. Then Ms. Meyer said, "We have heard about three holidays, Kwanzaa, Hanukkah, and Christmas. Who can tell us some of the things about these holidays that are the same?"

"You eat good food!" called Marty.

"You give and get presents," said Anna.

"You have parties for your family and friends," said Alicia.

"You light candles," said Paul.

"Nine candles in a menorah!" said Willie.

"Seven candles in a kinara," said Anna.

"Five candles in an Advent wreath," said Sara.

"Good for you!" said Ms. Meyer. "The holidays are the same in some ways and different in others. Each of these holidays is a happy celebration, and one of the nicest things we can do is share our holidays with one another."

Ms. Meyer put a menorah, a kinara, and an Advent wreath by the window. Then she pulled down the shades and turned off the lights.

She lit one candle in the darkness. She passed the candle to Sara. Sara used it to light a candle in the kinara. Then Willie got a turn to light a candle in the Advent wreath. Anna lit a candle in the menorah. Everyone got a turn to light a candle.

When all the candles were glowing, Ms. Meyer asked everyone to hold hands. Then she taught them a song she wrote:

Holiday lights,
See them shine.
Let's celebrate holidays,
Yours and mine.

Ms. Meyer turned the lights back on. "It's time for the surprise," she said. "And the surprise is a party!"

"Yes!" "All right!" "Yay!" the kids shouted.

It was a great party! It started at noon with surprise visits from parents bringing holiday foods. There was turkey and cranberry sauce. Potato pancakes. African fruit punch.

They sang songs and told stories. They played games. The party went on all afternoon.

When it was time to go home, Ms. Meyer's class had full bellies and were tired and happy.

As they left, they called to one another, "Merry Christmas! Happy Hanukkah! Harambee!"

HARRY'S HORRIBLE HOLIDAY GIFT

by Suzy Kline

A RADIO PLAY CREATED FROM THE BOOK

HORRIBLE HARRY AND THE HOLIDAZE

In a radio play there are no sets or props. The actors read their lines into a microphone. The sound-effects person has a microphone, too.

You can use pretend microphones for this play.

CAST OF PLAYERS

NARRATOR	MARY
CLASS	SIDNEY
MISS MACKLE	DOUG
HARRY	IDA
ZUZU	SONG LEE
DEXTER	SFX *(sound-effects person)*

(SFX needs cellophane, noisy wrapping paper, tape, and sleigh bells.)

NARRATOR: It is the last week in December before holiday recess. Room 3B has already done activities about Hanukkah, Kwanzaa, Three Kings Day, and the Korean New Year. Now the class is celebrating Christmas. They have made wreaths out of pinecones, decorated a class tree, and made up a song.

CLASS *(to the tune of "Jingle Bells"):*

Holidays! Holidays!

They're for me and you!

Christmas, Kwanzaa,

Three Kings Day,

And Ha-nuk-kah, too-oo!

NARRATOR: Room 3B's favorite Christmas activity is Secret Santas! The teacher, Miss Mackle, picks up a big glass jar that is on her desk.

MISS MACKLE: Boys and girls, each one of you is going to be a Secret Santa. You're going to give a gift to someone in our room. When you pick a name from this jar, you'll find out who it is. Your special gift will be a white elephant from your house. I want you to wrap it up and bring it to school by Friday.

ZUZU: What's a white elephant, Miss Mackle?

MISS MACKLE: Anything used that is still good. Like a puzzle with all the pieces. Or a toy that isn't broken. A book you've read. White elephants are things like that.

DEXTER: I got it! Like an old Elvis Presley record.

HARRY: I know what I'm going to give! It's something I've been keeping in the basement for months! It's underneath the bottom step.

MARY: Ohhhh, Harry! I bet it's something horrible!

SIDNEY: I bet it's something creepy!

NARRATOR: ZuZu doesn't understand. He is a new student in Room 3B and doesn't know Harry that well.

ZUZU: Does Harry give horrible gifts?

CLASS: Yes!

HARRY: *(cackles)*

SONG LEE: *(giggles)*

MISS MACKLE: Okay, boys and girls. Let's begin drawing names!

NARRATOR: Sidney picks a name first. We all

know who it is because he looks right at Mary.

SIDNEY: Rats! I wanted ZuZu's name.

MISS MACKLE: Now, Sidney. Please keep the name you drew a secret.

NARRATOR: It takes ten minutes for everyone to draw a name out of the jar. When it's time for recess, Harry and Doug race to the Dumpster.

HARRY: Whose name did you draw, Doug?

DOUG: We're not supposed to tell, Harry!

HARRY: No one will know. If we do the pinky-finger shake, we can promise to keep it a secret. We won't even tell our grandparents.

DOUG: Well . . .

HARRY: Come on, Doug. I have Dexter. Who do you have?

DOUG: Oh. . . okay. It's Song Lee.

HARRY: Song Lee? Yes! That's just who I was

hoping for. Want to trade names? I have a white elephant that only Song Lee will appreciate.

DOUG: I don't know, Harry. Are you giving a horrible gift?

HARRY: No! It's just . . . smelly. Song Lee will love it!

DOUG: Is it like perfume or something?

HARRY: Kind of. You'll see!

NARRATOR: Harry and Doug do their pinky-finger shake. When Friday finally arrives, everyone brings wrapped gifts to Room 3B and puts them under the Christmas tree. The class is excited to find out who their Secret Santas are.

MISS MACKLE: I have peppermint candy canes for each one of you.

SFX: *(crinkles cellophane)*

CLASS: Thank you, Miss Mackle.

MISS MACKLE: It's time to open the Secret Santa gifts. I'll pick a name out of the jar to see who goes first. ZuZu!

NARRATOR: ZuZu finds his gift under the tree. When he opens the card, he reads it.

ZuZu: For ZuZu and JouJou,

    I'm glad you're in our class.

    Happy Holidays!

               Song Lee

NARRATOR: ZuZu unwraps the gift.

SFX: *(rips some paper)*

ZuZu: Oh, thank you, Song Lee! JouJou will love these!

NARRATOR: We all look at the white-elephant gift. It's a stack of three different-colored pet bowls for ZuZu's guinea pig.

SONG LEE: They used to belong to my salamander, Chungju.

NARRATOR: Mary's turn is next.

MARY: *(groans)* Ohhh. I know this is from Sidney.

SFX: *(rips some paper)*

NARRATOR: When Mary opens the box, her face lights up.

MARY: A big chocolate cupcake? Yummy! But . . . where's the white elephant?

SIDNEY: Take a bite, Mary. But be careful!

NARRATOR: Mary took a small bite of the chocolate cupcake. She saw something inside!

MARY: Oh, how cute! It's that tiny good-luck doll you found in your slice of King Cake we had last week.

SIDNEY: Right!

MARY: I love it! Thank you! Thank you!

IDA: Did the little doll bring you good luck, Sid?

SIDNEY: It sure did! When I slipped on our icy

steps this week, I didn't break one bone. Just bruised my buns. That's what I call good luck!

IDA and MARY: Yay!

NARRATOR: Doug is next.

SFX: *(rips some paper)*

DOUG: It's from Ida. Wow! What a cool hat. I'm putting it on right now.

IDA: It's a kufi. It belonged to my uncle when he lived in Africa. He said I could give it to you.

DOUG: I still have the paper kufi we made in class, but this is much better! Thanks, Ida. I love it!

NARRATOR: Everyone has to wait to find out what horrible gift Harry gave. Song Lee's name is the last one drawn out of the jar. ZuZu is leaning forward to watch her unwrap the present. He's really curious about Harry's gift.

SFX: *(rips some paper)*

SONG LEE: It's from Harry, and it's heavy!

DEXTER: It has a funny shape.

SFX: *(rips some paper)*

SONG LEE: It has lots of tape.

SFX: *(rips some tape off paper)*

NARRATOR: When Song Lee finally finishes unwrapping the gift, she holds it up. It's a jar filled with something green.

SONG LEE: Ohhh! What's this green stuff?

HARRY: Read the note!

SONG LEE: Merry Christmas, Song Lee.

I hope you like this

holiday slime.

I sure like you.

Harry

NARRATOR: Song Lee unscrews the lid. A terrible odor fills the room.

CLASS: Eweeyeee!

SIDNEY: That stuff stinks like skunks!

HARRY: It's awesome. It's holiday slime!

MARY: It's a horrible gift!

NARRATOR: Song Lee pours a little into the palm of her hand. When she puts some between her fingers and rubs them together, the slime turns to powder.

CLASS: Eweeyeee!

NARRATOR: Song Lee doesn't complain. She just smiles!

SONG LEE: Thank you, Harry. This is like the green slime you made in class last year with cornstarch and water.

HARRY: Yup! But this is a batch I made last summer. I kept it in a jar under the basement stairs. All I had to do was add a little more water.

MARY: No wonder it smells so bad! It's been fermenting for five months!

SIDNEY: P.U.!

MISS MACKLE: Well, it is a festive green for Christmas!

ZUZU: It's really neat! It's two states of matter. It pours like a liquid and turns hard like a solid.

SONG LEE: *(giggles)* I like it, Harry. It's stinky fun.

HARRY: I knew you would appreciate it, Song Lee. I think ZuZu does, too!

NARRATOR: After the class eats their candy canes, Harry makes up another verse. He rings sleigh bells while his classmates sing his new words.

SFX: *(rings sleigh bells)*

CLASS *(to the tune of "Jingle Bells")*:

Room 3B

Room 3B

We're what everybody wants.

We've got bells

And stinky smells

And share white elephants!

A SOLDIER'S CHRISTMAS

by Sue Wright

Johnny and his father and mother were sitting around the kitchen table one Saturday morning. It was a few weeks before Christmas. Mom had something important — a new e-mail from Johnny's big brother, Tom. Tom was a private first class in the army. He sent an e-mail every week. This one had come late the night before.

Dear Mom, Dad, and Johnny, I'm fine. Hope you are, too. It is windy and cold in the desert tonight but that feels better than daytime. Days are hot with no breeze.

Guess what, Dad? When we're not on sniper patrols, I'm learning to play chess! Another PFC has started a chess club. Chess is a little hard for me so far, but I like it. Makes me think of checkers, only for smart people.

How about you guys? Are you ready for Christmas yet? What do you want from Santa, Johnny? You'll have to wait for a present from me—all of you. I haven't had a chance to buy anything, but I do have some great ideas.

The sergeant warned us yesterday not to expect much in the way of Christmas celebrations while we're on high alert. There's too much to do. Whether we get Christmas dinner with all the fixings will depend on what's going on with the war and where we're based.

I know that wherever I am I will be thinking of you and remembering all the special Christmases I had at home. Good-bye for now. I'll write again next week. Love, Tom

Mom passed the e-mail around, and Dad and Johnny both read it again. Johnny was always glad to get letters from his big brother. He missed Tom a lot. So did Mom and Dad.

After breakfast Mr. Roberts put on his jacket. "See you later," he said. He waved good-bye as he went out the door to do errands.

Mom turned to Johnny and said, "I've got an idea of what we can send Tom for Christmas. It will be a big surprise." She got up and headed for the basement door. "Want to come along?" she asked.

Johnny jumped out of his seat. "Sure! What kind of surprise?"

"You'll see," Mom said. She opened the door, and they went down the stairs to the basement.

Mom went to the shelf where they kept the Christmas decorations — six boxes of them. The biggest, heaviest one was marked CHRIST-MAS HODGEPODGE.

The hodgepodge box was filled with old toys and decorations. The box had not been opened for two years, not since Mrs. Roberts had gone on a "Christmas Homes" tour. All the houses were fancy, modern homes, trimmed with shiny silver and gold decorations.

"Our decorations are really out of style," she

told her family after the tour. "It's time we moved into the twenty-first century."

Tom was still home then. One day he and Johnny were upset to find an eight-foot-tall purple plastic Christmas tree in a corner of the living room. They had always had a fresh-cut pine.

Their father wasn't happy, either. "Does this mean we aren't going to the Snowflake Christmas-Tree Farm like we always do? What about our ride in the farm's horse-drawn sleigh?" he asked.

"That's so old-fashioned. We've done it so many times. This year will be different," Mrs. Roberts announced.

Mrs. Roberts kept her promise. Instead of a sleigh ride and the hot chocolate they always enjoyed, the boys had to dress up in Sunday clothes and go to some dumb Christmas ballet about a nutcracker.

After all their complaining, the ballet had been okay. Otherwise, Tom said, their mom might have found a rubber snake in her Christmas stocking.

The brothers were pretty sure their mother would want to decorate the new purple Christmas tree herself. But she didn't have the heart to take the job away from them. So just like every other Christmas, the boys were asked to hang the ornaments on the tree.

The ornaments his mother had bought were the ugliest things Johnny had ever seen. She had gotten them in a store where even she had to admit, "Only a space alien would feel at home."

"They're so flimsy!" Johnny said. He broke

two of the space-age ornaments just getting them out of the box. His big brother, Tom, broke three. They hid the broken pieces at the bottom of the trash can.

Luckily their mother hadn't noticed anything. She was too busy arranging the new glass and brass Christmas decorations.

After the decorating was done, Tom and Johnny had looked around. Everything was hard and shiny, and the colors were weird. No red and green anywhere. "Why is she doing this?" Tom asked their father. "Does Mom want to make our family a laughing-stock?"

Right after Christmas, Tom joined the army and was shipped overseas.

It was funny — well, maybe more sad than funny. This year, Johnny's mom had hardly mentioned Christmas. Nobody in the family had, not even Johnny. They just couldn't stop worrying about Johnny's brother being in the war. Maybe going through the hodgepodge box would make things better. Johnny hoped so.

Johnny's mother sat on the floor and opened the big box. "Oh, look!" she said. "It's poor old Santa Claus."

"Santy!" Johnny cried. "I've missed you!"

Johnny shook the little beanbag Santa to rearrange its beans, and gave it a sniff. "He smells like Christmas, Mom," he said. Then he tossed the toy to his mother the same way he and Tom had tossed it back and forth for so many Christmases.

Mrs. Roberts took a whiff. "That's because your Santy's been lying next to this bayberry candle for two years — along with these cookie tins."

This made Johnny remember something. "Since we have the tins, will you fill them with those Christmas cookies you used to make? I promise not to eat all the frosting before you ice the cookies."

"It's a deal," Johnny's mother said. "But you also have to promise me that you'll sprinkle the colored sugar on — without getting it all over the floor. Sunday we'll play a Christmas CD and spend all afternoon listening to Christmas music and making Christmas cookies. How does that sound?"

"Perfect!" Johnny answered. He was glad that his mom wanted to listen to Christmas music. A few days ago they had been listening to the radio when some Christmas carols came on. She had asked him to change the station. The songs had made her think of Tom being so far away for the holidays. Johnny had seen tears in her eyes. But now she seemed to be in the mood for Christmas after all.

Johnny watched as his mother pulled a bag of silver tinsel out of the hodgepodge box.

"Ha!" she said. "This is what we need. We had brass icicles on the tree last year. Maybe this year we'll turn the clock back and go old-fashioned again."

"I vote for that," Johnny said. "I like the old stuff best — like this angel."

"Do you remember when this angel used to be at the top of our tree, Johnny?"

"You mean when our tree was green, Mom? Sure."

Mrs. Roberts laughed. "This angel has been in the family for a long, long time. It's a little dingy and the left wing needs to be sewn, but I bet old Harold still has a few good years of tree-toppin' left in him."

"Harold?" asked Johnny.

"That's what I nicknamed him when I was a kid," his mother said.

Johnny thought that was strange. "An angel named Harold?"

"What else?" his mother said, and she began to sing "Hark! The Herald Angels Sing."

Johnny laughed along with his mother.

"Mom," he said, "can we have a green tree this year, with real ornaments?"

Mrs. Roberts reached out and fluffed Johnny's hair. "Absolutely, dear! A green tree trimmed with nothing but decorations from the hodgepodge box."

The laughing stopped as his mother reached into the box again. Suddenly, she looked more serious.

"I think this is what I've been looking for," she said. "The perfect gift for your brother."

Mrs. Roberts held a tiny object in her hand. It was wrapped in tissue paper. Slowly she pulled the paper away and held out her hand for Johnny to see.

Johnny smiled. "Tom always loved this," he said.

"Come on," Mrs. Roberts said as she got to her feet. "We need to get it in the mail right away."

"Wait," said Johnny. He picked out a couple other things.

"Good idea," his mother said. "We'll put those in the package, too. Let's hurry and wrap them."

On Christmas Eve a few weeks later, Mrs. Roberts checked the computer. There was an e-mail! She printed it out and carried it into the living room. Johnny and his father were sitting on the sofa looking at the beautiful green Christmas tree. It was covered with the old ornaments and silver tinsel; Harold was at the very top.

Johnny's mother read the e-mail:

Dear Mom, Dad, and Johnny, The guns are quiet tonight and for that I am thankful — for the little baby in a matchbox manger, too. I was so surprised and happy to see him again. I keep him in a secret pocket of my uniform.

I've been playing with Grandpa's reindeer whistle and my Frosty the Snowman yo-yo — that is, when I can get them away from my buddies.

Where did you find the manger and the

toys? They must have been in the hodgepodge box.

I hope to see you guys real soon. Sarge says our unit should be home by Easter. I'm counting on it. Johnny, please put some Christmas cookies in the freezer for me — if they aren't already all gone. And hey, don't forget to give the tree a drink. Remember, a green Christmas tree needs lots of water.

Merry Christmas, dear family! I love you, Tom

TWO OLD CHRISTMAS CAROLS

HARK! THE HERALD ANGELS SING

Words by Charles Wesley, 1739

Hark! The herald angels sing,

"Glory to the newborn King;

Peace on earth, and mercy mild,

God and sinners reconciled."

Joyful, all ye nations rise,

Join the triumph of the skies;

With the angelic host proclaim,

"Christ is born in Bethlehem!"

Hark the herald angels sing,

"Glory to the newborn King!"

A *herald* is "a person who brings news." The herald angels bring news about the birth of Jesus. *Reconciled* means "brought together." *Proclaim* means "to tell."

O LITTLE TOWN OF BETHLEHEM

Words by Phillips Brooks, 1867

O little town of Bethlehem,

    how still we see thee lie.

Above the deep and dreamless sleep,

    the silent stars go by.

Yet in thy dark streets shineth

    the everlasting Light;

The hopes and fears of all the years

    are met in thee tonight.

For Christ is born of Mary,

    and gathered all above,

While mortals sleep, the angels keep

    their watch of wondering love.

O morning stars together

    proclaim the holy birth,

And praises sing to God the King,

    and peace to men on earth!

WALLY'S CHRISTMAS IN THE CITY

by Barbara Seuling

Jingle bells, jingle bells . . . The music came across the car radio.

"Jingle bells, shmingle bells," said Lindsey's dad, at the wheel. "I think it's a bad idea to bring a big dog like Wally into the city."

"Oh, don't be a grouch, Daddy," said Lindsey. "It just wouldn't be Christmas if we put Wally in a kennel."

Kennel! What about the kennel? Is that where we're going now? Wally's stomach whooshed. He had been in a kennel once, when the family had to go away for a weekend. The dog in the next cage had whined all through the night, the food wasn't the kind he was used to, and, worst of all, he didn't have Lindsey's bed to curl up on at night.

"Dad! Stop the car! Wally's going to be sick!"

The car jiggled slightly, but kept on going. "Lindsey, I can't stop now. We're on the George Washington Bridge!"

"That's okay," said Lindsey. "It's too late, anyway." Her dad groaned, while she did her best to clean up with a roll of paper towels and a pint of bottled water.

They drove up to a tall building with an awning over it. Wally stared. *This isn't the kennel.*

Did they make a mistake? Lindsey opened the door and he jumped out. "Wally!" Lindsey yelled, jumping out after him, waving the leash. "Wait a minute."

How can I wait? I've got to go! Wally went right for the tree in front of the building. It was not in the ground like most trees. This one grew in a box. A man in a uniform with gold buttons down the front ran out, waving his finger. "Naughty dog!" he said. Wally's ears went back. Uh-oh. He was off to a bad start.

Lindsey's mom apologized as they filed into the building. Wally's toenails *click, click, clicked* on the hard marble floor. Didn't they have any dirt in the city? He missed dirt.

"I told you the city is no place for a dog," said Lindsey's dad, as they crowded into a tiny room.

"It will be fine," Lindsey said. "People who live in the city have dogs, too."

The door slid closed, and Wally felt the room move. He flattened himself onto the floor. Moments later, the door slid open again.

"Here we are, " said Lindsey's mom, opening another door with a key. They went inside.

Wally went to the window to look out. There was no street out there, just another building with lots of windows. He moved closer to see better. The street was far below. He dropped down on his belly and backed away with a low whine.

"What's the matter, Wally?" asked Lindsey. "Don't you like being on the twelfth floor?" Lindsey scratched his ears. "This is Aunt Sue's apartment. We're staying here Christmas week while I'm off from school and she's having a vacation in Barbados. You'll get used to it."

A week? A whole week? Wally lay on the floor by a big soft couch. He didn't think he'd get used to it, but he couldn't let Lindsey know. She had begged her parents to take him along instead of putting him in the kennel. She didn't even do that for the cat. Old Mrs. Harvey was taking care of him.

"I'm going out for the Christmas tree," said Lindsey's dad, "before it gets dark. Tonight we can decorate it."

Christmas tree? Not again! Didn't they remember the last time they had one of those? Wally remembered. They had stood a tree in the living room and hung all sorts of sparkly things on it. Then he knocked it down when he chased the cat. He thought the family would send him back to the Safe Haven Doggy Shelter after that, but for some reason, they let him stay.

"Mom, can I take Wally for a walk while

Dad's getting the tree?" asked Lindsey. "Central Park is right across the street."

A walk! Now you're talking! Wally jumped up and headed for the door.

"Yes," said Lindsey's mom, "but you can't go alone."

"Why not?" asked Lindsey.

"Because you're only eight years old and this is New York City. I'm going with you."

Wally didn't like being on a leash, but Lindsey said they had no choice. This was Central Park. It was huge, and he could get lost. For a moment, he yearned to be in his own backyard, chasing squirrels.

As they entered the big park, Wally saw people walking, riding bicycles, pushing carriages, and running. The smells were good, too. Someone had dropped a piece of hot dog and he swept it up with his tongue. But best of all, there was dirt! Just for fun, he started scratching, sending some flying into the air.

When he looked up again, Wally saw a bunch of people in the distance standing around with lots of dogs playing near them. He made a beeline for them, pulling the leash out of Lindsey's hand.

Wally didn't stop until he reached the dogs. Then he turned to look. Lindsey and her mom were running toward him and shouting.

Uh-oh. What have I done now? Before he could think, a little schnauzer leaped out at him and snapped. Wally jumped back and ran, dragging the loose leash behind him.

"No, Wally, wait!" shouted Lindsey. Wally turned again, and this time some of the dog people and their dogs had joined in the chase.

"Stop!" "Wait!" "Come back!" they shouted. The dogs ran beside them.

Why are they all after me? Wally couldn't figure out what he had done, but he'd better get out of there. He ran until he didn't hear the shouting anymore. He stopped to catch his breath.

Looking back, he saw no people, no dogs. He had finally lost them. What would he do now? He wandered around, lonely and a little bit afraid. Maybe he'd let Lindsey find him, even if she was mad at him. But he looked around and there was no Lindsey.

In the distance, he saw little lights like the kind that were on their Christmas tree last year. He heard voices and followed them.

The lights were wrapped around trees outside a fancy building. A car had driven up and a man in a red jacket with gold buttons helped people out of it. He held the door open as they walked into the building. Wally went closer. Maybe Lindsey was there.

"Shoo!" said the man in the red jacket, coming out again and chasing Wally away. *What was it about people wearing gold buttons?*

Wally wandered along a wide path until he got to a small building that was all closed up. Rowboats were not in the water but stacked upside down on the shore of a big lake. He sniffed the ground for something to eat. That little piece of hot dog had not done much to fill him.

Still sniffing, Wally walked along the path. He came to a bridge arching over the path and checked around — no food, but it was dry here and felt safe. He dropped down next to the wall of the bridge and curled himself into a tight coil, resting his chin on his paws. *Where is Lindsey? Will I ever see her again?* He thought of the happy sounds in the house when everyone was wrapping presents. He could almost hear them singing now: *"Jingle bells, jingle bells . . ."*

". . . Jingle all the way . . ."

Wait. That *was* real singing. And it was close by. Wally's ears shot up. A man and two kids about the same size as Lindsey, bundled up in heavy jackets and woolen hats and scarves, were singing as they approached the bridge.

"Look! There's a dog!" he said.

"You think that's the one?" said one of the shorter ones, a boy.

"Must be him. He's got a leash on."

The three of them walked up to Wally quietly, speaking softly. Wally was so homesick for Lindsey that his guard was down. Before he knew it, the man grabbed the leash. They turned back the way they had come. Wally was trapped.

Where are they taking me? Why didn't I run when I had the chance? I never should have run from Lindsey. Wally wondered how he would ever find Lindsey now. Maybe her dad had been right: The city was no place for a dog.

They walked some distance before they took a turn and saw a row of buildings, standing tall against the sky, over the trees. Wally saw a figure in a red jacket. Uh-oh. Was that the man with the gold buttons? He tried to get away, but the man held tight to the leash.

Wally looked again. Could it be? It looked a little like . . . It was! . . . Lindsey! And Lindsey's mom, too! They were running toward him. No matter what he had done and what the punishment would be, he would face up to it. Anything to be back with his family.

"That's my dog!" said Lindsey, coming to a halt in front of them.

"He was under the bridge up ahead," said the man. "We passed you before when you were looking for your dog. We thought he might be yours."

"Thanks!" said Lindsey, taking the leash from the man. "Thanks so much." She wiped her eyes with a mittened hand.

"Sure," said the man, "and Merry Christmas." The kids echoed the greeting.

The words sounded perfect to Wally. He jumped up and licked Lindsey's face. It was salty. She had been crying. *Was I that bad that I made her cry?* He licked her hand to say he was sorry.

Lindsey knelt down and hugged Wally, tears still streaming down her face. "Boy, you had me scared."

What? You were scared? What about me? He didn't even want to think about it.

On the way home, Wally walked so close to Lindsey, he almost didn't need a leash. He wasn't going anywhere!

They passed the cluster of dogs and people again and Lindsey waved.

"Glad you found him!" someone shouted.

"See you tomorrow," shouted another. "Merry Christmas!"

"Merry Christmas," Lindsey and her mom called out at the same time.

A golden retriever came sauntering over, wearing a big red bow around her fluffy neck. Wally's tail wagged like it would fly off. The dog planted a kiss on his nose with a big lick and went back to the others. Wally's heart beat faster. That felt really nice. Maybe he'd see her again tomorrow. Central Park wasn't bad. It was just a bigger backyard, that's all.

Wally was beginning to get this Christmas

thing. Maybe he didn't know all about it yet, but he knew it made you feel good, like when things turned out all right after you were scared, or when you were welcome in a place that was unfamiliar to you, or when your family was all together, no matter where that was.

Like the way he felt right now.

A VISIT FROM
ST. NICHOLAS

by Clement Clarke Moore, 1822

'Twas the night before Christmas,
  when all through the house
Not a creature was stirring,
  not even a mouse.
The stockings were hung by the
  chimney with care,
In hopes that St. Nicholas soon
  would be there.

The children were nestled all snug
  in their beds,
While visions of sugar-plums
  danced in their heads.
And Mamma in her 'kerchief, and I
  in my cap,
Had just settled our brains
  for a long winter's nap;

When out on the lawn there arose
  such a clatter,
I sprang from my bed
  to see what was the matter.
Away to the window I flew like a flash,
Tore open the shutters
  and threw up the sash.

The moon on the breast of the
  new-fallen snow,

Gave the lustre of mid-day to objects below,

When, what to my wondering eyes
  should appear,

But a miniature sleigh, and eight tiny
  reindeer.

With a little old driver, so lively
  and quick,

I knew in a moment it must be
  St. Nick.

More rapid than eagles his coursers
  they came,

And he whistled, and shouted, and called
  them by name:

"Now, Dasher! Now, Dancer! Now, Prancer
  and Vixen!

On, Comet! On, Cupid! On, Donder
  and Blitzen!

To the top of the porch! To the top of the

  wall!

Now dash away! Dash away! Dash away

  all!"

As dry leaves that before the wild

  hurricane fly,

When they meet with an obstacle, mount

  to the sky;

So up to the house-top the coursers they flew,

With a sleigh full of toys, and St. Nicholas too.

And then in a twinkling, I heard on the

  roof,

The prancing and pawing of each little hoof.

As I drew in my head, and was turning

  around,

Down the chimney St. Nicholas came with

  a bound.

He was dressed all in fur, from his head

  to his foot,

And his clothes were all tarnished with

  ashes and soot;

A bundle of toys he had flung on his back,

And he looked like a peddler just opening

  his pack.

His eyes — how they twinkled! His dimples,

  how merry!

His cheeks were like roses, his nose like

  a cherry!

His droll little mouth was drawn up like

  a bow,

And the beard of his chin was as white

  as the snow;

The stump of a pipe he held tight in his

  teeth,

And the smoke, it encircled his head

  like a wreath;

He had a broad face and a little round belly,

  that shook when he laughed, like a bowl full

  of jelly.

He was chubby and plump, a right jolly

  old elf,

And I laughed when I saw him,

  in spite of myself.

A wink of his eye and a twist of his head,

Soon gave me to know I had nothing

  to dread.

He spoke not a word, but went straight

  to his work,

And fill'd all the stockings; then turned

  with a jerk,

And laying his finger aside of his nose,
And giving a nod, up the chimney he rose.

He sprang to his sleigh, to his team gave a
  whistle,
And away they all flew like the down of a
  thistle.
But I heard him exclaim, ere he drove
  out of sight,
"Happy Christmas to all and to all
  a good night."